Fifty
or More

*More observations and fictions about life
through short stories and poetry*

Chris Lihou

© 2025 Chris Lihou

FIFTY or More: More observations and fictions about life through short stories and poetry

First edition, May 2025

Nifty Fifty Publishing
Qualicum Beach, British Columbia
cplihou@gmail.com

FIFTY or More: More observations and fictions about life via short stories and poetry is under copyright protection. No part of this book may be used or reproduced in any manner whatsoever without written permission except in the case of brief quotations embodied in critical articles and reviews. All rights reserved.

This is a work of fiction. Names, characters, businesses, places, events, locales, and incidents are either the products of the author's imagination or used in a fictitious manner. Any resemblance to actual persons, living or dead, or actual events is purely coincidental.

ISBN: 978-1-0694207-0-1

Dedicated to my wife, my two daughters and my four grandchildren.

Acknowledgements

I'd like to acknowledge the support of my wife Anne, who encourages me to pursue my writing passion and supports the idea of committing my work to this book.

I'd like also to acknowledge the help, encouragement, and support of Cindy Folk, my publishing advisor.

Contents

- Introduction 1
  - 1–The Flash 3
- Failure 3
- Lost 6
- Alien Illegals 9
- Cigarettes 14
- Patient Zero 15
- Be Yourself 16
- Passion 17
- Jupiter Street 18
- The Taste of You (1) 19
- The Taste of You (2) 19
- The Taste of You (3) 20
- The Taste of You (4) 21
- Smoke Break 21
- Closing Time 22
- Road Train 23
- Love's Web 24
- Until the Next Time 25
- The Fall 28
- Christian Louboutin Shoes 30
- Chris 2.0 31
- Widow? 33
- Silence 34

Fertility 37
Tuesday Funk 39
Art School 40
Steve's Mussels 43
Deception 45
   2–The Dribbles 47
Lemons 47
Twinkly Lights 47
Wish 48
Global Economy 48
Mist 49
Book Box 49
The Last Coin 50
Finer Grind 50
Paid Maid 51
Sweets 51
Mirror Be Damned 52
Alibi 52
Raise Up 53
The Codes of Life 53
Women 54
Promissory Notes 54
A Case for Auto Correct? 55
They Noticed 55
Climate or Weather 56

Alex(a) 56
Our Last Hike 57
Novelty is a Powerful Aphrodisiac 57
Last Minute Fears 57
Landfill 58
Sadness 58
Flowers 59
Wash Day 59
The Method 60
Frugal Fran 60
Sirens 61
Daily Routine 61
The Front Man 61
Expenses 62
The Waiting Room 62
Loyalty Programme 63
Summer Love 63
Back Then 64
Bad Day 64
The Power of Music 64
Rebel 65
Role Play 65
Autumn 66
Autumn 2 66
Autumn 3 66

Mrs. P. 67
Dark Shadows 67
Counting the Sleeps 67
Violet 68
Release 68
On Hold 69
Forgotten 69
Losing it 70
Eejit 70
The Lawn 70
Not Much Cop 71
Balancing Act 71
Diagnosis Delivered 72
DIY 72
Stories 73
An Old Love 73
Patina 74
Migrants 74
Autumn's Traffic Lights 75
   3–The Drabbles 77
Signs of Silliness 77
Moving 78
Knock on the Door 78
Big Hitter 79
Now is Not the Time 79

Skipping Stones 80
First Massage 81
Cemetery 81
Moving On 82
Her Thighs 82
The Corset.. 83
Headwinds.. 83
Memories 84
Earring Stud 85
Risk and Reward 85
Bedtime Conversations 86
Time's Up 87
Choice   87
Downsizing 88
Noises... 88
Best Laid Plans 89
Prescription 89
Dead End.. 90
First a Kiss 91
The Importance of Hair...................................... 91
Holes 92
Pockets 92
In Hot Water 93
A Night with the Boys 93
First Impression 94

Synchronicity	94
One Letter	95
The Passing of Time	96
Code Flags	96
Intergenerational Trauma	97
Welcome	97
Wet Dreams	98
4–The Poems	99
Hat	99
River	100
Love's Name	101
Did You	102
Coal Black	103
Tethered towards Extinction	104
Time Traveler	105
Steed	105
Knight	106
Shadows	107
Worry	108
Night Silence	110
Our Past Lives	111
Pseudo-Science	112
Tired	112
Perhaps	113
There	116

Oh! Canada 117
  Publishing History 118
  About the Author 120

"There is something delicious about writing the first words of a story. You never quite know where they'll take you." —Beatrix Potter

Introduction

According to Wikipedia, Flash fiction is a brief fictional narrative that offers character and plot development.

Identified varieties, many of them defined by word count, include the six-word story; the 280-character story (also known as "twitterature"); the "dribble" (also known as the "minisaga", 50 words); the "drabble" (also known as "microfiction", 100 words); "sudden fiction" (up to 750 words); "flash fiction" (up to 1,000 words); and "microstory".

Some commentators have suggested that flash fiction possesses a unique literary quality in its ability to hint at or imply a larger story.

For the purposes of this book, I've not used these divisions exactly.

Chapter 1, The Flash contains stories that are longer than those in the other chapters.

Chapter 2, The Dribbles contains stories of approximately 50 words in length.

Chapter 3, The Drabbles contains stories of approximately 100 words in length.

1–The Flash

Failure

Since his teenage years, Alan had failed.

His failure was not simply a matter of lacking coordination, like tripping over his feet. No, it was a bigger, more persistent type of shortcoming; the sense that inadequacy had seeped into his whole being, even before any specific setback happened. A sense of uselessness weighed so heavily it caused him to always be hunched over, eyes looking down to his feet. He knew that he was insufficient because he heard it from his father, his schoolteachers, and his soccer coach. The kids at school reinforced the message and made no secret that they considered him a loser.

At his peril, he repeatedly neglected to learn protective lessons from his mistakes. Time and time again, he did not keep quiet whenever he disagreed with his father. Such an omission caused immediate and unpleasant consequences. He was subjected to abuse.

"*Alan has once again failed to reach his potential*," his teachers recorded on his annual school record. That also had consequences. He did not graduate.

His coach said he did not run fast enough or tackle the opposing side vigorously enough to help his side win. That, too, had consequences. He was booted off the team.

Even his advances to one of his teammates ended in an embarrassing failure. He was ineffective at being gay.

One day, he had had enough. At the local hardware store, Alan purchased a length of tumble dryer hose. Driving his car to a remote spot, he connected one end of the hose to the tailpipe and the other end he passed through the window. He then sat in the car with the engine running and the radio playing his favourite music. On his phone, he typed a message. *"I've had enough and no longer wish to live this miserable life."* Before he could finish the message, there was a tap on the window. A dog walker disrupted his intentions.

He had failed in his attempt at suicide.

There was no doubt about it; Alan could see that he was good at only one thing: failure.

Despite being prescribed anti-depressants, Alan lived as a friendless, petulant, anti-social person, addicted to his smartphone.

Unexpectedly, this last behavioural characteristic proved to be a salvation. One day, he watched an influencer on his phone talking about taking whatever you do best and turning it into a career path. This caused Alan to think that since failure was his most developed skill, he would write a book covering all he knew about the subject.

For the next ten months, he became even more anti-social and sat at his desk and wrote, page after page, until he had written eighty thousand words or so about the subject he knew best. Alan gave the work the title "*How I Was Successful at Failure.*" As expected, when he thought he was finished writing, and in keeping with his experience, Alan did not succeed in getting the draft manuscript accepted. Despite being accustomed to a lack of success, he somehow found the fortitude to persevere. With his seventeenth submission, Alan received his only positive response from a small, upstart publisher where the editor offered to collaborate with him to make the manuscript publishable. Two years later, his book was in the bookstores, and he embarked on a small promotional speaking tour.

His message: "*Do not give up hope; creative success can spring from abject failure.*"

His books sold in modest numbers with a message that seemed to resonate with his audience. Alan had found his tribe; his eyes sparkled, and his shoulders no longer slumped. He responded to an approach from one of his readers, and they began dating.

Failure, it seems, had given Alan a life no longer dominated by failure. He's thinking about his next book.

Lost

Sophia's hood on her navy-coloured jacket was pulled over her head, and her eyes were directed towards her feet. She was out walking and needed to ensure a secure footing on the uneven cobbled pavement where the smooth, dark stones glistened from the recent rainfall. Significant rainwater was flowing noisily in the gutter, heading downhill to the nearest sewer grating. With her head down, Sophia received a modicum of protection against the chilly, blustery November wind stinging her face.

To her right, she saw an inviting sign in a shop door's window. "Why not stop in for a coffee?" Despite her wet weather clothing, she was cold, and the greyness of the day had done little to lift her spirits. Under the circumstances, the warming impact of a hot coffee would be most welcome.

Sophia depressed the lever and opened the glazed wooden door with her right hand. It creaked as she pushed it forward. Just inside, at the cash register to her left, sat a young man with a hippy-like appearance—mangy, braided, unkempt hair and full beard. He barely acknowledged her arrival, so engrossed was he with the computer screen in front of him. "Where's the coffee?" she asked. "Upstairs at the back," he replied without looking up, leaving her on her own to figure out any further directions. She manoeuvred herself past the piles of books on the floor. Each pile had a pink Post-It note on top, presumably recording what was planned for them next. The shop had a distinct smell of age, musty and dusty.

Where it existed, the carpeting had patches worn right down to the backing. Where it didn't, old, worn and bare pine floorboards could be seen. The aisles themselves were very narrow; passing other shoppers would be a challenge, not that she could see anyone in the store but herself. The shelving, bulging under the weight of books, went all the way from the floor to the ceiling, making it impossible to see beyond the aisle in which she was standing. No natural light appeared to enter the aisles. The store was thus a warren of dimly lit passages, a maze with no obvious beginning or end.

As she entered the first aisle, labelled Fiction A-F, the muffled voices started. From above her, she heard a deep, echoing voice say, *"It doesn't matter who you are or what you look like, so long as somebody loves you."* She froze.

Unsettled, Sophia quickly went to the end of the first aisle and entered the adjacent one, Fiction G-M, only to hear another voice: *"When you play the Game of Thrones, you win, or you die."*

Quickening her stride, she went into another aisle. The old wooden floorboards flexed and squeaked beneath her feet. Fiction N-S. Another voice! *"Who controls the past controls the future. Who controls the present controls the past."*

Where are these voices? What is this place?

Sophia was all but running now, lost in the maze of passages. Where was the exit? She wanted out. She took the uneven, carpeted but threadbare stairs two at a time. She got a glimpse of a window and headed in that direction. Before she reached the door, she heard yet another voice sounding almost like a preacher, *"All we can know is that we know nothing."*

She was agitated. Her pulse raced. Finally, she found the door, but not before she heard one last voice, a resonant echo from the end of a tunnel: *"The real world is where the monsters are."*

Fresh air! She gasped. Gulped. She looked back at the sign above the door. Frank's Books, Est. 1910, New and Used, **Audio Book Specialist**, a fact she hadn't noticed when she entered. She wished she'd never visited.

"It doesn't matter who you are or what you look like, so long as somebody loves you." —Roald Dahl, *The Witches*.

"When you play the game of thrones, you win or you die." —George R. R. Martin, *A Game of Thrones*.

"Who controls the past controls the future. Who controls the present controls the past." —George Orwell, *Nineteen Eighty-Four*.

"All we can know is that we know nothing. And that's the height of human wisdom." —Leo Tolstoy, *War and Peace*.

"The real world is where the monsters are." —*Rick Riordan, The Lightning Thief.*

Alien Illegals

They appeared on the southern beach aboard a burnt orange floating object of perhaps some four metres in length. The craft was barely able to hold the four rotund individuals clear of the water. While neither the mode of the craft's propulsion nor its steering mechanism was evident, the vessel nonetheless moved purposefully and steadily towards the coastline on what was a particularly calm day. It would not require an experienced boater to notice that without the calm water in the English Channel, the craft would surely have become swamped, so low was its freeboard. The newspapers had been reporting overloaded inflatables sinking and lives lost in the past few months, even as the flow of migrants making the perilous journey had been unrelenting.

When the craft noisily crunched onto the beach pebbles, its occupants stepped ashore, each dressed in matching and rather curious garb, the same colour as their craft. Their apparel was not unlike the hooded, one-piece pajamas that very young children wear to bed. The hoods of those coming ashore obscured their faces, so it was impossible to gain any sense of their origin. Short red boots on their stocky legs offered protection from the cold water as they stepped out of their craft.

Once ashore, the four collectively dragged the craft out of the water while speaking to each other in a very curious, African Xhoisan-like language, comprising a rapid series of clicks.

Having observed these events, two immigration officials accompanied by two police officers moved down the cobbled beach to greet them. This was becoming a common event. Illegal migrants seeking asylum regularly chose this particular gently sloping beach as a landing place, so officials were almost always on hand to greet them.

It had become increasingly difficult for the officials to show concern and empathy. They were under pressure from their political masters to slow the flow of illegal arrivals. Their usual 'greeting' was overly abrupt politeness followed by stern instructions.

Despite the communication difficulty and the officious treatment directed towards them, the four latest arrivals remained passive and seemed inquisitive of their new surroundings.

Using hand signals, the officials herded the four into the rear of a white, unmarked van at the top of the beach so that they could be transported to the nearby Migrant Processing Centre (MPC).

Within the hour, having arrived at its destination, the receiving MPC officials opened the van doors.

They found the van empty! Only four wet patches indicated any prior occupation.

The resulting paperwork and any reasonable explanation for four "lost" individuals was now going to be a massive headache for MPC officials and their Home Office masters.

What made matters worse was that a member of the public had observed the arrival of the strange craft. He was out walking his black retriever, and on seeing four hooded persons the dog growled and tugged at his leash, causing his owner to pay close attention to unfolding events. After they were loaded into the van, he phoned his nephew, Sidney Philips, a freelance journalist known for his obsession with the paranormal.

"Hello, Sydney. I thought you'd be interested in what I've just seen—four very odd-looking chaps arrived on the beach just now in an unusual orange craft. They were wearing strange clothes too. The MPC officials have now taken them away to the holding centre."

Sidney was intrigued by what he heard and rushed to the beach to investigate. Speaking with the MPC staff, he found them hesitant to provide details out of concern for their credibility. But it was clear to Sydney something had happened that was far from the norm for migrant landings on this beach. It was also clear that there were no survivors associated with the abandoned craft. After concluding his few enquiries and receiving a formal "No Comment" from MPC officials, Sydney put out a story of the mysterious disappearances of four illegal arrivals at the hands of the MPC.

The story did not stop there. The next day an official response was made public.

The communique read—*"Due to privacy concerns, we cannot respond regarding individual cases, but we'd like to reassure the public that the Department does all it can to respect the rights of individuals arriving illegally on our shores. Yesterday's case was no different."*

Sydney knew denial and obscuration when it was delivered. It only served to heighten his journalistic inquisitiveness, which led him to uncover a connection he could not ignore.

He had picked up on Reuters that at almost the same GMT, a rather similar occurrence was reported to have occurred at a crossing of the Rio Grande from Mexico into the USA. Apparently, a certain Wayne DeSota, a bilingual agent with Customs and Border Protection, reported that four individuals wearing orange hoodies had tried to traverse the Rio Grande into the United States. When the suspects failed to respond to directions from officials in either English or Mexican and continued their journey into the USA, they were shot. On approaching the bodies, Wayne reportedly said that the bodies were nowhere to be seen despite extensive searches. Only their abandoned, orange landing craft remained.

Even more curious for Sidney was yet another report he unearthed. At a similar time, a patrol aircraft reported sighting four individuals in a small orange craft in the Timor Sea and within Australian waters.

No further reports had been lodged as to what happened next.

Sydney had a penchant for writing about haunted buildings, UFO sightings, and, more recently, his belief in the existence of extraterrestrial visitors to Earth. So, he put all these reports together, and international news picked up his resulting story under the headline, "Immigration Measures Tested by Alien Scouts."

Sidney's story suggested that these events were all linked and the disappearing migrants were alien scouts. He further suggested these scouts had quickly determined and communicated with each other that the world was not a friendly place to outsiders and had simultaneously returned whence they came. Moreover, and in keeping with his paranormal enthusiasm, he speculated that this was not the first time the Earth had seen extraterrestrial visitors.

Cigarettes

A voice boomed with a thick Scottish accent: "Welcome ta eternity, Reginald."

Ye've paid the ultimate price for yer wee addiction ta cigarettes.

Behind ye is a flight of ten thousand steps ta yer new hame–a place reserved for those who deid from their tairrible addictions–booze; cigarettes, cocaine, an' the like. Once ye arrive, ye an' yer co-inhabitants have the freedom ta indulge yer particular addiction … forever.

However, before ye start the arduous ascent, we're able ta offer ye a one-time special deal. If ye accept, ye'll become a ghost takin' trips inta the real world ta frighten mortals inta givin' up their addiction. Each successful intervention will earn ye points for good behaviour, an' with sufficient points we will allow yer special privileges–wee indulgences ta spice up yer eternal existence.

So, Reginald, what you gonna do? Will yer stride up those steps or take this braw chance ta become a ghaist an' start yer new posthumous existence by scaring yer ain bairn out o' his fatal drug habit?"

Patient Zero

Consumed with fever, Bruce lay in his bed. With his eyes wide open, he could not see it, but with his eyes shut, he sensed the menace, felt it, his pulse thumped in his neck, his skin bristled, he could smell his unpleasant, rank sweat seeping out from his pores.

The translucent horror he saw moved towards him, walking–if indeed it was a walk—right through him, enveloping him into itself in the process. All the solidness that was Bruce vanished. Before his sight disappeared, he could see clearly through his now transparent hands. His throat was constricted, unable to release a scream of terror. He became as a jellyfish, oozing from the bed onto the floor, slipping under the door and beyond, destined to absorb other victims.

Bruce Allen, deceased, was retrospectively assessed as patient zero of the latest creeping, body-devouring virus that spread throughout the population via the feet of the unsuspecting.

Be Yourself

Growing up, Paul was told what to think, what to wear, what to want, what to be. Parents, schools, family, society, advertisers, were all eager, persuasive, rule-bound participants in their never-ending pursuit of confirmation bias, whose "*Become what you want to be*" Paul saw as an obvious, hypocritical and wholly unconvincing, contradictory narrative.

Years later, Paula chose to live alone, off-grid, free from societal shackles, becoming a renowned creative painter and science fiction writer. A creator of fictional worlds where nonconforming beings existed without preconceived and imposed notions of normality.

The works resonated with those who felt similarly oppressed but were less brave in their lived response, and were valued by wealthy conformist art directors as creations from a very talented artist.

Passion

Unlike yesterday, she now lay relaxed, naked, wanting to receive, to share, waiting to give of herself so as to meet her lover's desires and their mutual attraction.

Yesterday, in contrast, her lustfulness thrust itself into her daytime consciousness, demanding it be quenched. This primal urge had been so insistent she sought out a male escort whose magnificent erect phallus she proceeded to use as if it were simply a dildo, without any regard for the muscular body engaged in the coupling, frantically riding it until she was fully sated before showering away any telltale signs and calmly returning to her office.

With her urgency so recently tamed, tonight, she would luxuriate in the act, taking time to feel and be felt, to love and be loved and, at its conclusion, to absorb the full sereneness of the afterglow.

Jupiter Street

The message said the dashboard GPS device needed updating. Frank hit *update,* and continued driving. The GPS screen went blank for the next ten or so kilometres before it came alive again. Frank pulled over and punched in the street name–Jupiter—not that he needed directions, he'd been there many times before, but he wanted to be sure the update was functioning. The device took a few seconds and indicated he should proceed straight ahead. Then it directed him left down a gravel road he'd not used before. As Frank turned the corner, he lost control of the vehicle on the pea gravel.

Frank's next awareness was of being prone, with a strange, white-cloaked figure looking down on him, the face and head obscured by a hood. "Hello," it said. "Welcome to Jupiter, your home for eternity."

The Taste of You (1)

The infatuation has stimulated my senses. I hardly recognise myself. Even the coffee I'm drinking in this café, the one where we first met, tastes better.

I'm tingling, aware of your presence, the glint in those Mediterranean sky-blue eyes as you approach, wisps of your blonde hair spilling across your face, your smile, a glimmer of white, surrounded by crimson, suggestive lips. I'm unable to forget the soft, sweet apple taste of your parting kiss that has left me wanting to have it forever.

You head to the booth opposite. He plants a kiss on your cheek.

My life is over!

The Taste of You (2)

The phone rings. I see the number. The caller ID tells me who it is. I hesitate. My emotions have so recently been in turmoil. I was elated, besotted, and then you ignored me. Then he kissed you on the cheek. I've lost all semblance of positivity. Bottles are piling up on the coffee table next to the takeaway Uber Eats food cartons. I've called in sick.

If I pick up the phone, will I just hear why you broke up with me? I already hurt enough. But it is one last chance to hear your voice.

"Hello?"

"Look, I'm sorry about yesterday. I didn't want my brother to know about us. He thinks I'm still happily married. Brian's away until Sunday. If you cook dinner tonight, I'll bring the wine."

The Taste of You (3)

The buzzer rings. I can see her via the door camera. I let Jessica into the building. As she is being lifted seven floors in the elevator to my apartment, so, too, are my spirits, despite the day's grey clouds and light rain.

I've had a crazy couple of hours, making the flat presentable after my lovestruck funk. I've had to shop for dinner ingredients and refresh the bedroom and bathroom linen.

A few minutes pass, and Jessica knocks gently on the door. I open it and see her smile, her long, yellow, curly hair and black raincoat glistening with fresh raindrops. From a sizeable shoulder bag, she produces a bottle of wine that I take, kissing her on the cheek in return, just as I saw her brother do yesterday. The huge grin suggests she gets my joke.

"Let me take your bag and coat."

She hands me the bag and then drops the raincoat to the floor. She is wearing nothing but a bra and panties. Jessica takes my hand and leads me straight to the bedroom. "I want to make it up to you," she says.

The Taste of You (4)

I'm now back at work.

Two days have passed since Jessica walked into my apartment in only her underwear. Two days since she spent two nights and much of the daytime in my bed. Two days since lust and the physicality between us were all that mattered. My mind and body retain an aching and vivid imprint of our time together.

Now, I'm totally at the mercy of those memories as I await Jessica's next call, Jessica's next freedom.

Why did I allow myself to get involved with a married woman?

I should know. I am one.

Smoke Break

In more affluent neighbourhoods, it would be called a porch.

In this locale, on the side of a decades-old, weathered, stucco home, it is simply a large flat surface at the top of four steps, providing level access to the side door of the house.

On this platform is a very tired, 1950s chrome chair with torn, red vinyl. A woman in a housecoat is perched on the chair, with her hair tied tightly in a bun, an outcast from the house while she smoked a cigarette. When the fag was finished, she rested her head in her hands, considering something, a weighty concern needing support.

The wooden screen door opens. A small child yells, "Mummy, Daddy has come home drunk again."

Break over.

Closing Time

His time was inexorably coming to a close.

Whenever he can, he sits and naps in a chair behind the window through which the sun provides nurturing greenhouse warmth.

He reflects on his life, trying to get the measure of it.

What if he had it over again, would he choose as he did? Would Heather? Grace had been a loving partner, but even after all the years had passed, he still had thoughts for Heather.

And the kids, could he have done differently by them? The pursuit of his career meant financial security for the family, but at the cost of precious little time with the children growing up.

His life, perhaps all lives, seemed to have unfolded from a series of little decisions, the outcome of which was unpredictable at the time of their making.

Now he knew the outcomes, and it was with that improved knowledge that he had cause to wonder in those last few restful hours in the sun.

Road Train

Gazza, a veteran trucker, walked slowly around his juggernaut–a six hundred horsepower road train. His experienced eye, on the lookout for anything amiss, carefully scanned the three trailers, eighty tyres and the cargo of one hundred and forty-four cows. He'd made this journey before, so he knew it would be foolish to be complacent before crossing the hot, dusty desert. Gazza wanted a trouble-free trip. If all went well, he expected to be in Alice on Wednesday, considering the required stops to water his cargo and give them their mandated rest.

Seeing nothing of concern, Gazza stretched a leg onto the step and pulled himself into the cab. He settled into his familiar air-sprung, air-cooled seat and turned on the diesel, the instrumentation flickering to life. He was ready; he wound the window down and yelled "Hooroo!" to the grazier, who waved back from his Belgium-sized station. Slowly, the juggernaut inched forward.

As the station passed into his rear-view mirror, he saw a bright light falling towards the rusty red earth alongside the heat-induced shimmering black highway. "A meteorite?" he wondered, slowing the rig to a stop. He stepped down and began searching the scrubland.

"Probably space junk," he mused. Then it edged towards him. "Holy Shit," Gazza blurted out. With pulse racing, he ran back to his cab.

From the vantage point of the driver's seat, he could see the object, only now there was the object he'd first seen plus four animal-like creatures, each growing in size, as though being re-hydrated. The four moved towards the road. In the shimmering heat of the tarmacadam, they stopped and melted into four glistening puddles. "No one is going to believe this."

He turned towards where the initial object had been, but it was already gone.

Love's Web

The necklace—a single large amber jewel gripped by platinum fingers and suspended on a delicate silver chain—held within its solidified resin a dark trace from the past: a tiny prehistoric spider, eternally suspended in a sticky situation.

Jane cherished the necklace, wearing it daily. It echoed her chosen profession of archaeology, but its true meaning, and her reason for wearing it, was its parallel to her ongoing love for a married man—her university professor. In her final year, she had been caught up in a furious, fraught, but intense web of illicit love and passion–a love that has remained despite the relationship's painful break-up two years prior.

Now, at the uncovered site of a Roman fortification, she works on her knees, carefully scraping the dust and detritus from fragments of history, trying to make sense of antiquity.

All the while, her neck holds another fragment–a powerful and meaningful reminder of her sticky past.

Until the Next Time[1]

What a night! What a party! Stumbling home with a mouth that feels like sandpaper to my tongue and with a residual taste of vindaloo, I seek out a late-night drug store.

My frazzled brain screams for something to counteract the excessive drink. I look at the counter, unable to make a choice: pain relief or stomach relief, vitamins, or rehydration fluids—or all of them.

I'm amazed to see a leprechaun sitting on the shelf beside the paracetamol. I rub my eyes in disbelief,

---

[1] Each week Authors Only Collective (AOC) has a prompt for the weekend. The first part of this story was submitted in response to "You walk into an all-night pharmacy at midnight and run into a mythical creature."

but he's still there–a little man in a green jacket, short green trousers, a green hat and sporting a bushy red beard. "Go home," he tells me. "Have a full Irish breakfast: bacon, sausages, eggs (scrambled or fried), white pudding, a grilled tomato, beans, mushrooms, hash browns, plus toast with butter and jam."

I rush out of the store and vomit in the street at the thought of such a disgusting meal and decide I'm never going to drink again.

At least not until the next time.

I return to the drugstore. At the same counter, the little green leprechaun mockingly says, "Hello again, eejit." I tell him to bugger off and pick up two bottles of a very unnatural blue fluid full of electrolytes. The cashier was grateful for the Plexiglas screen when I paid, shielding him from the unpleasantness of my inebriated state.

Outside, I gargle the first mouthful of blueness and quickly drink the rest of the bottle. The second bottle defied my uncoordinated ability to open it, so with an expletive, I throw it, narrowly missing my intended lamppost target—and stagger homeward.

As I lurch along, I become increasingly alarmed at the prospect of my live-in girlfriend Alice's reaction to my arrival—if she is awake.

Of course, Alice will be awake! She's seen me inebriated before and would not be surprised to find me sleeping it off on the couch. But, like a truffle-seeking Lagotto Romagnolo dog, I'm concerned that she will detect the scent of another woman buried beneath my musk of booze, smoke, body odour and vindaloo.

Earlier in the evening, Amanda and I had found ourselves in a comfortable corner where silly, drink-fuelled jokes progressed to a full-on snog. She gave approving moans through our attached mouths as my hand reached under her blouse to locate her breast. Embarrassingly, her hand on my crotch found me with a brewer's droop, which prematurely ended our coupling; Amanda pulled away–"Another time, eh, John!"

I consoled myself with a final pint of Guinness and left. As I did so, I caught a glimpse of Amanda with the young Shaun Ferris. Maybe she'll have better luck with him.

I arrive and fumble, eventually finding the key to open the door to the staircase leading to my first-floor flat. There seem to be more stairs than I remember. As I reach the last step, I trip, keys clattering to the concrete floor. I attempt to stand, but my knees seem unable to accommodate my weighty frame. I crawl to my front door, sensing a warm liquid on my chin, my tongue tasting blood from a split lip. And then I see that damn leprechaun again, watching me as I struggle. "You bloody eejit." I tell him to "fuck off" and unlock the flat door, closing it as quickly as I can to leave the little bastard outside.

I recall nothing until a whisper in my ear says, "Would you like a black coffee?" I'm lying on the couch, fully clothed, feeling like yesterday's, warmed-over, bubble and squeak. A nod from me gets a mug of the hot, obsidian liquid deliberately slammed loudly onto the coffee table next to the leprechaun–how did he get in here? The little man says to me, "She knows, eejit."

Alice angrily adds–"Quite the night, eh, John, you idiot? When you are clearer headed, you had better have a fucking good story to tell me about that woman you were with."

The Fall

John was on an errand for bread and milk. Without the latter, his necessary cup of joe—and, thus, his day—would not begin well. He had a morning routine established over many decades. Without his coffee–well, who knows what might happen?

The village store was a fifteen-minute walk or a three-minute drive from the cottage. Today, there was no choice as the car was being repaired after an unfortunate interaction with a stubborn sheep on a single-track lane.

The vehicle was repairable, the sheep not so much, becoming a bonus for the local butcher.

It was cold. Frost covered the land and the roofs. The whiteness gave the gently sloping fields a sparkle in the early morning light, adding to the palette of autumn's last colours: golden yellow in the hazel trees on the field boundaries.

Despite his hip being arthritic and painful in the cold, he hurried home for the coffee and the warmth provided by the wood-burning range. Underfoot, the fallen leaves crunched with each step, and the ice-covered indentations crackled as he stepped on them.

It was on one of these that he tumbled. His hasty steps lost traction–the bread trapped between John and the hard, frozen ground. Under his weighty frame, the loaf resembled a pancake.

The milk fortunately remained in its container.

Arriving at the cottage, he was still swearing to himself, which continued until the coffee was ready.

Alongside his caffeine fix the flattened bread would become a late breakfast, fried in bacon fat.

John's day would undoubtedly improve although the pain and the embarrassment would take a while to diminish.

Christian Louboutin Shoes

It was one of the best of autumn days. The calm and mirror-like sea reflected the pale blue sunny sky, where tufts of individual white clouds sat in layers upon invisible surfaces. Each cloud had a flat, translucent blue-grey base rising to an intense fluffy whiteness at the top.

Sandra ceased her cloud gazing and looked along the beach towards the chalky cliffs and beyond. She then peered down at her feet; an act necessary to avoid falling as she began to move forward.

Walking with this downward-looking posture gave her the hunched appearance of an old woman bearing all of life's burdens. She could see her bare, misshapen toes, crooked with age and arthritis, leaving strange, twisted imprints in the cool, damp sand.

Despite years of taking advice and wearing sensible shoes, she could see that the long-term outcome for her now crooked feet had always been inevitable.

But oh, how she now wished she'd ignored that sober advice and worn those glamourous, bedroom-beckoning beauties with pencil-thin high heels and red soles whenever she felt so inclined–if only she had danced more, unrestrained by prudence. If only she could have enticed the handsome, charming Tom—with his warm, welcoming brown eyes—to be her paramour. Tom, the then Junior Minister destined for even greater political appointments. Tom, the only one she found to set her emotions alight. It had been a lonely wait all these years, hoping another suitor would ignite her flames. Lonely because she had been too afraid to take a risk.

If only she had worn those shoes.

Chris 2.0

"Would you like to install the update tonight?"

Oh yes, please! I'd love an update.

A reboot to remove aches and pains, with a software refresh to sharpen memory and boost energy levels.

Second thoughts: Let's not wait until tonight–do it now.

> *"First, please agree to our terms and conditions:*
>
> *1. You absolve the provider of all or any adverse consequences arising from your participation. For example, some participants have noticed a desire for their old selves. Others have experienced sharpened recall of previously unpleasant,*

> *hidden memories. These should be short-term effects. Please revert to your backup if they persist.*
> 2. *You agree to back up your existing memory before installing the update.*
> 3. *You agree to the one-time fee of $109 or a membership to our fitness club for $59 per month."*

Agree. One-time update. Next.

> *"Please provide your contact email and payment details.*
>
> *Payment accepted. A non-refundable update file has been sent to the email address on file. If your update doesn't work, try turning yourself off and on again.*
>
> *Good luck. Remember to use your backup if necessary."*

One-time update received, along with backup instructions. Commence backup.

Memory backed up. Update started. The spinning wheel appears. Oh, shit! How do I Force Quit to re-install backup?

How do I turn myself off and on?

Widow?

The harbour is little more than a breakwater–a wall of granite boulders offering scant protection against the relentless forces of the northern Atlantic. A short row of cottages sits on the rise above, each with a commanding view of the tiny harbour and beyond.

Beneath roofs of black slate, the cottages were built decades before from stones hewn of local grey granite. From their chimneys, puffs of smoke blow horizontally away from the coastline—the smouldering peat within providing only a modicum of comfort.

Dry stone walls mark each property boundary. The walls provide some solace for such plantings as are huddled in their lee. All growth struggles—stunted, leaning away from the onslaught of the westerlies. No trees are in evidence, only the occasional stubborn, prostrate shrubbery clinging to the thin soil amidst a carpet of moss and lichen.

Behind a window in one of the small cottages sits a woman, staring longingly out to sea. She tries to keep warm with her shoulders draped in a hand-woven shawl.

To venture outside in today's conditions requires a hunched posture into the face of the blustery, salt-laden wind—a mirror to the tenacious, bent-over shrubs. As on similar days, the wind whistles and howls, relentlessly probing to locate access into the cottage via any crevice that might exist around doors or windows. Before trickling down to the sill, droplets of saltwater spray pummel the salt-encrusted window glass like tiny shotgun pellets.

The woman's view to the horizon is of white spumes violently torn from the dark and ominous chaotic sea. She huddles on the dry side of the glass, hands cradling a mug of something warm. Anxiously, she waits and hopes to see his boat return, dreading that nature's relentless force might make her a widow today—like many fishermen's wives before her.

In the distance, she now sees a mast making a fleeting but recurrent appearance as a boat rides the up and down of the waves. She stares with increased intensity, hoping it is the "Seawitch" headed for home. Eventually, her fears recede as she recognises the blue-hulled craft. Smiling, she heads to place more peat on the fire. Tonight, there will be a sweet reunion and fresh fish for supper.

Silence

I'm agitated and unsettled by my unspoken thoughts. My skin bristles and I'm flushed with fresh desire as memories of Tom fill my mind. In these dark early hours of the night, thoughts that cannot be spoken torment me. *Will I always love two men at the same time?*

John is breathing heavily by my side, unaware of my internal conflict. Although I've not seen Tom since John came into my life, his memories persist in my silence, and the physical desire to be with him feels overwhelming. I want to call him, to be touched by him. Unlike me, his marriage survived our passionate affair. He could not, would not, leave his wife. I, on the other hand, would have given up everything to be with him. Indeed, I did give up my first husband. Then, on the rebound, I found John, a good man but sadly without the incredible sexual allure of Tom.

Oh! Tom, whose smile makes me blush as though I was standing naked before him, whose eyes know that my nipples are already firm and erect beneath layers of clothing, whose touch on my shoulder produces electric sparks to my groin, whose presence beside me causes me to lose clarity of thought or speech and who magnifies my every sexual urge.

I'm now on my way to work. John has left early to catch a plane for a two-day business trip. I'm still thinking about Tom as I drive. I call his number hands-free and then cancel the call before it is connected. I'm conflicted; my breathing becomes laboured; I'm feeling anxious. I try again, this time allowing the call to connect.

"Hi Tom; Sonia."

"I recognise your voice."

I'm panting now, having difficulty articulating my desire. "I... I need to see you. Just... just one more time. No drama, I promise."

By the time I reached the office parking lot, it was decided–we would meet at the restaurant where it all began. The evening would echo our first encounter: wordless and heavy with magnetic physical charge.

As we planned, nothing was said throughout the meal. Seated across from each other, only our eyes and grins spoke of our mutual desire. We took turns feeding each other throughout the four-course chef's menu, sharing from a bottle of sparkling red to loosen our inhibitions and heighten anticipation.

The ride to the motel was equally silent, heavy with unspoken yet familiar expectations. Once inside, he selected slow cello music on his iPhone and led me by the hand to the bedroom. I undressed slowly and provocatively to the tempo of the emotive rhythm and submissively laid back on the bed as I'd done so many times before.

As our coupling progressed, our voices broke the silence, emitting non-verbal sounds of love understood in any language, until we were both replete and again silent.

We each accepted the truth. As we agreed, the evening had mirrored our first, but our affair was now over, bookended by erotic silence. Our liaison had been an intense interlude of powerful, passionate urges matched only by equally fiery arguments. The relationship had met our powerful physical needs, but it had left its scars, unravelled lives, and ultimately led to my antagonistic divorce. Both my first husband and now the beautiful, charismatic, beguiling, sexually magnetic Tom were out of my life.

I dressed and quietly let myself out of the motel room. I paused momentarily at the door looking back for the last time. We had made so many memories and satisfied our needs and desires. All that was now over.

I walked away, returning to my other life tortured by two regrets: one, that the affair with Tom was over, and two, that by ending the affair with this last fling, I had just betrayed my current husband.

But has my affair truly ended? Tom's hold on me is still all-consuming. Could he truly be out of my life?

It is not lost on me that I have yet to decide about taking the morning-after pill.

Fertility

Women in Shinga held Nuala in reverence; some even thought she might have special powers since her crops thrived, even as others grew poorly.

Each week in the growing season, Nuala, accompanied by her loyal companion, Whisker, the cat, pushed her cart on the dirt track to the market to sell whatever was ready to harvest from the small plot of land she tended. Having no store in which to sell her produce, she sold her vegetables directly from her cart. It gave Nuala a meagre income, a whisker above starvation, but she accepted it, just as her mother and her grandmother had done.

The season before, Fricka had stopped Nuala and poked her produce until she found what she wanted. Fricka, older than other single women in the village, lived alone and was known for her disagreeable disposition, finding negative or critical things to say about everything in all her conversations.

Nuala pleaded with her to take a particular crescent-shaped squash, shorter and uglier than the one she had chosen. Fricka dismissively ran her hand over the squash. "It's far too crooked," she complained. "It may be unsightly," said Nuala, "but I guarantee it will be full of fertile seeds for you to plant. Just as you will surely find a husband and have many children."

Fricka reluctantly heeded Nuala's advice, and as if by magic, this season she had both a husband and a child, which she ascribed to Nuala's powers.

Since then, a murmur passed throughout the women of Shinga that Nuala had the power of matchmaking and fertility. Even more women desired Nuala's vegetables and her magical power to find a husband. Now she routinely sells out her cart and dispenses magic before arriving at the market.

Tuesday Funk

Tuesday.

Again.

I'm a "regular" here so Jock knows the drill and pulls me a pint of my "usual" without being asked.

The brown brew mirrors my mood–dark and bitter. Bubbles rise chaotically to form the creamy head on the drink–swirling to the surface like my own internal turbulence.

June, Jock's wife and my former lover, gives me a sly, knowing smile from behind the bar. Everything in my life seems to be *former*—former husband, former lover, former manager, former abstainer.

I don't think Jock knows about June and me. My past intimacy with her makes it hard to meet his eyes but Jock senses my mood. No words pass between us. I give him a nod, and he pulls a second pint, as I rush to down the first.

The last time I felt like this was when my wife left.

Of course, she had every reason to leave when she found out about me and June. Soon after, June saw me more clearly too. She recognised I wasn't a rising star–just a loser. And she wasn't a groupie, screwing a soon-to-be famous author.

Today's deep funk?

Yet another publisher rejected the manuscript that took me a year to write. I've not found the courage to read the latest feedback. Perhaps I will after I leave the bar, sufficiently fortified.

Meanwhile, self-doubt crashes over me like storm waves on a shingle beach–noisy, relentless. Without an anchor I'm drifting in my own negativity, no calm refuge in sight.

I cling to the glass–my only friend. The smooth, vitamin-rich Irish brew provides both nourishment and pain relief–relief from the rejection by women and editors. Maybe the brew will give me enough courage to begin my next novel.

Until then, I'm in good literary company–just another drunk, just another would-be author.

Art School

Most of her peers worked at bars, accepting tips and drinks from men who made unwelcome, lewd remarks towards their youthful prettiness. Others worked at restaurants and coffee shops accepting tips in return for enduring the leering of men's eyes that undressed them as orders were taken.

But attending art school and living away from home was expensive.

Even so, Sarah refused to supplement her own funds by working at the establishments her colleagues had chosen. Drunken males and their intemperate comments held no interest for her. But Sarah needed to find a source of funds to pay for food and rent, which sorely tested her resolve to avoid the easy money available in the service industry. Then, a small advertisement caught her eye:

Wanted–models for life drawing and sculpture classes.

As a result, Sarah began taking payment for posing naked in front of students who silently manipulated clay to replicate her body. In the hushed tones of the studio, she was not subjected to unwelcome remarks. The only voice Sarah heard was her own, internal, lustful thoughts as she strived to remain motionless.

Beneath their intense gaze, she felt the hands smoothing and squeezing the cool grey clay as if it were her own flesh. Holding their full attention imbued her with a feeling of control and power. Thankfully, unlike the opposite sex, her arousal at the thought of their hands was her invisible secret. Not until she got home to her digs did she release her anticipation and tension, as her own hand, and those of the imagined sculpture students, became one.

By the end of term, the students in the class knew Sarah's body as intimately as if each of them had shared her bed. In fact, Sarah was intimate with only one; Melanie, who seemed able to both sculpt her contours and connect with Sarah at a deeper level. Melanie's skilled hands were as masterful on the flesh of her muse as they were on cold clay. In

Melanie's company, Sarah no longer felt under artistic scrutiny. She relinquished power and control. In return she received support and love.

Being intimate with Melanie changed how she responded to the students. For them she was professional, poised, detached but otherwise unmoved on the inside. But when her lover was present in the room, her naked stance became a provocative pose, while internally she surged with sensual excitement. Between their eyes passed unspoken but understood messages of desire. On such days their mutual passion was infused and heightened by these hours of silent foreplay earlier in the studio.

Sarah's artwork became ever more prodigious and was frequently permeated with erotic imagery during her time with Melanie. It was as though her union with Melanie was an amphetamine stimulant. While Sarah was Melanie's muse for Melanie's course work in the sculpture studio, Melanie became a muse for Sarah's sensual black and white images in the photo lab, outside or in the bedroom–work that went well beyond the requirements of Sarah's course curriculum.

A small showing of Sarah's work at a local gallery was both well received and condemned for its provocative, pornographic like images. Sarah embraced the controversy and was spurred on to create more pieces for public consumption and outrage.

The outrage eventually brought her national attention when a local newspaper reported on a protestor who sprayed white paint across the "naughty bits" of her photographs on display at a gallery.

This became a transformative incident for Sarah. She used the technique of white spray paint herself to creatively obscure elements of her photographic work–which became a signature element of her work that was in turn, in much demand.

Sarah's success, which had so often included obscured images of Melanie, became a point of increasing tension between the lovers. As Sarah sought to produce fresh work, she engaged others to be her models. Melanie's jealousy eventually gave rise to their acrimonious separation.

Sarah never finished her studies and continues to produce commercially successful artwork. Melanie graduated, moved to the country, raised two children and produces sculpture in her spare time.

Steve's Mussels

Steve invited Suzanne, tempting her with a home-cooked meal. They'd discovered a shared love for good food, which became the basis of their burgeoning relationship.

Kissing Suzanne gently on the cheek, he left her alone, beside a smooth, well-weathered log.

Suzanne tried to relax with her back supported by the log, randomly doodling in the dry sand as she contemplated their relationship. She was slowly learning a little more about Steve who appeared so calm and reassuring in comparison to other men she'd been out with. She really liked him, but was unsure if she should continue to see him.

Today's tide had fully retreated. It was the lowest tide of the year. Large patches of sandy mud filled the spaces between the exposed, mollusc-covered rocks–acres of seafloor normally covered with water. Now exposed, the mud emitted an acidly pungent smell–sulphurous, anaerobic, reminiscent of rotten eggs.

Steve was near the water's edge, collecting large blue-black mussels from the rocks and depositing them into a square plastic pail. Moules marinière was on tonight's menu. His interest in cooking, combined with his love of the outdoors, meant that he had developed an enjoyable habit of foraging—mussels at low tide, chanterelles from the woods, wild garlic, spruce tips, berries, nettles, and more.

Suzanne had recently learned that Steve had a nine-year-old son. She wasn't expecting that. While this news was disquieting, what troubled her most was that Steve also told her he'd served time for fraud. Like the retreating tide before her, Steve's past was slowly emerging and, like the exposed mud, his past life had an air of unpleasantness.

She wondered if she could trust him. But for now, she put off any decision. She was thinking about the meal.

Deception

It's been six months since Mum died. In truth, as her mind became increasingly ravaged by dementia, she'd not been with us for much longer.

Today, as on every Sunday morning since her death, I'm by her graveside, talking to her, tending the weeds and replacing the wilted flowers. It's become a ritual. The cemetery offers a peace that I relish. Embarrassingly, I am also enjoying the fact that I'm no longer responsible for Mum's needs.

Of course, I'm holding a one-way conversation, like so many we had before she passed. I've an urgent question for her this morning. "Why didn't you tell me, Mum? I've a right to know."

I'd been sorting out her things and found a small tin box hidden behind dusty books on her bookshelf. The box's contents have captivated me since. There were letters–love letters addressed to her–plus a black and white photograph of a handsome airman in uniform. From the uniform and the letters, it's clear he's an American called Captain Bob Stewart. Robert. Stuart. My first names!

I've spent my spare time this week reading and re-reading the passionate letters, each infused with expressions of longing and desire. I'm sure Mum realised they'd eventually be found.

So, from beyond the grave, mother has spoken to me, albeit I've only got one side of the story. I've now got so many unanswered questions.

The letters are dated in the months before Mum married Dad. In the last one, Bob says he must return to the States, to his wife and young son, despite his love for Mum.

I've been working out dates and studying Bob's features. I've concluded I wasn't born early, just conceived early–and not by the Dad I've known. He died three years ago, likely unaware of Mum's deception while they were engaged.

2–The Dribbles

Lemons[2]

Countless lemons were sacrificed for the cause. Young teenagers surreptitiously pass seemingly blank pieces of paper to each other during class.

The ruse continued into college as their feelings crystallized. Bitter lemons became sweet words of love under heat. Choosing to be partners, Mary and Ellen turned lemons into love.

Twinkly Lights

The light rainfall has now stopped. The small branches are devoid of leaves following the brisk December winds.

On the underside of the branches, sprinkled throughout the shrub, cling tiny globes of light, sparkling, convex mirrors.

My spirit soars at the sight of these; nature's very own Christmas twinkly lights.

---

[2] Writing with lemon juice is invisible until the paper is warmed.

Wish

It was black, very black. And silent.

Then the storm hit. Rain forcibly, noisily, peppered onto the windows.

Nature's fit of anger the only sound. No fridge hum, no furnace fan: just my worried breath and this predicted gale.

Power was out.

I so wished I'd replenished the torch batteries.

Global Economy[3]

They say that *home is where the heart is*.

Stan's international career meant he left a little of his heart in each of the places he worked, acquiring passports to three countries over time.

Now retired, Stan looks for a place to call home, where he can reassemble his heart.

---

[3] This is semi-autobiographical.

Mist

Mist descends, silently seeping, wetting everything.

Shivering, cold, moisture drips from hair, from eyebrows, from glasses. Brian can no longer run, no longer see a path.

Daylight morphs into grey light, soon to become dark light. Senses deprived, absent visual clues, sounds sucked away.

His dog's nose will become his exit guide.

Book Box

He built a community book box located at the bottom of the drive. "Take One, Leave One," said the sign.

So, they exchanged books over the following months, getting to know about each other's taste in literature.

After he left her a book by D.H. Lawrence, she visited his cottage.

The Last Coin[4]

A simple coin toss, its outcome interpreted as a calling from the divine.

Upon its result, Matteo entered the Franciscan monastery. As a friar, he would help the sick and the poor without worldly goods, working and begging for food.

Curiously, he had used a coin to eschew all coinage.

Finer Grind

A new grinder, a finer grind, same beans, totally altering the taste of coffee.

As the New Year's party approaches, Celia considers what other single modification could revise the taste of her life.

Celia decides.

From now on, Celia will no longer be narrowly defined. She/They become their preferred pronouns.

---

[4] I once met someone who used a coin flip for all her decisions, including what and how much she purchased at the grocery store.

Paid Maid

Mary dreaded these times. In fifteen minutes, he'd had his way with her and was now contentedly snoring.

Wide awake, she reflects on her now loveless marriage and inability to leave because of her monetary dependence.

No longer a loving wife, she feels like a paid maid and sex worker.

Sweets[5]

It was Saturday. Pocket money day.

As usual, Tim spent all of his at the sweet shop.

His sibling bought a comic and saved the change.

Fast forward twenty years. One sibling became a dentist; the other owns his own house outright.

Sweets are still a key factor in Tim's life.

---

[5] In the 1950's it was quite usual for children to spend all of their Saturday pocket money on sweets and comics. Rationing of sugar (and thus sweets/confectionery) ended in Britain in 1953.

Mirror Be Damned[6]

Mirror be damned, the image was wrong, like that of the long-deceased father. Clutches the phone, "Just Cuts? I'd like a cut and colour."

Following day, after a sensuous night at Dance 41, they overdosed.

Dead, unlike anyone familial. Now their true self: coiffured, earrings, rouge, lipstick. No person, no mirror, could mock them any longer.

Alibi

The ruse had been working.

Instead of eighteen holes each Friday, he played just nine and then left to meet with Susie. His golf buddies agreed to cover for him should questions arise.

---

[6] In this piece there is some ambiguity. I leave the reader unsure about several things. What sex assigned at birth is the person looking at the mirror? Presumably male as I mention the father. What is Dance 41? Presumably a night club. (This is an obscure reference to The Dance of the 41 in Mexico City, of an illegal police raid at a private dance in 1901 where 19 men were dressed as women.) Then, suddenly, I use the word 'they'. Oh! Possibly it's a non-binary person. Their true self—coiffured, and presumably in death, presenting as a female. Was the death accidental? Clearly, some degree of gender dysphoria is implied. Such fun to write on so many levels!

But his wife noticed that the golf course invoice showed a zero bar tab.

His alibi was shot.

Raise Up[7]

We raise our kids, our bread dough, our hands and voices to the Lord.

We raise our crops and flowers and funds for good causes.

We raise our buildings, our spirits, and our glasses in toast.

Then, when war happens, everything built by our opponents we raze to the ground.

The Codes of Life

Vacation over.

Four-digit code to enter house.
Four-digit code to turn off alarm.
Four-digit code to access voice mail.
Switch computer on–another code.

---

[7] This was written in response to the horrific images of the Israel/Palestine conflict. I was also intrigued to employ the use of homophone—raise and raze.

Outstanding bills–bank code plus two-factor verification code.

Now, relax, have coffee, read book *Bletchley Park: The Code Breaking Story of Alan Turing*.

Women

Artist Marcel surrounded himself with women. He needed them; they served his needs.

Women were his models, his mistresses, his housekeepers, his partners at the bordello, and the mother of his children.

Curiously, Marcel went to great lengths to ensure his daughters grew up independent and not subservient to men.

Promissory Notes[8]

You could give me promissory notes with Benjamin Franklin printed on them.

Or, with a marriage certificate, I could give you physical love, home-baked bread and even children in exchange for shelter and protection.

---

[8] A bank note is a promissory note. Benjamin Franklin's face is on US$100 notes.

It is your choice–pay as you go or make a long-term contract.

A Case for Auto Correct?

Her message: thx for ivite will c u 2nite

He replied: grate we can sip at mine be4 going out 2 dine.

She replied: Look4 me around 6 let the wine breathe be4handjob might make me late

His response: If v. late bring pizzand more cab sav c u later

They Noticed

They noticed. When they got together, they spoke of him, how he'd lost weight, something about his hair, his demeanour. Friends do that. Observe, comment, speculate. "Why?" they'd ask. Perhaps an undeclared illness?

Turns out they were right.

His illness was love. He was seen with a new woman yesterday.

Climate or Weather[9]

It's very, very cold.

A special weather statement is in effect–an arctic front brings minus forty degrees with the wind chill. Is this global warming?

I turn up the furnace by two degrees Celsius. It's comfortable, not catastrophic.

We directly experience weather, not climate–the PR challenge for scientists.

Alex(a)[10]

Alex was with his latest paramour. Back at his place, they were enjoying themselves. Claire was an enthusiastic and very vocal lover. As things heated up, she said loudly, "Yes; Yes, fuck me; Fuck me harder, Alex."

A voice from the bedside table replied, "Umm... I don't know that one."

---

[9] On a very cold January day I realised that besides the decreased trust existing for science there is a huge PR challenge to explain that which is unseen, unfelt and not experienced. Climate is not weather as we experience it in the here and now.
[10] Amazon speakers/Alexa are always listening!

Our Last Hike

We've been together for many odoriferous miles. Recently, we tramped through ice-covered puddles in the shade and their liquid-only cousins in the sunny parts. Unfortunately, the effects of wear finally appeared. Squelchy, icy cold water seeped through my left sole. I will shop for my replacements before my next hike.

Novelty is a Powerful Aphrodisiac

In the continual pursuit of new experiences, Felix climbed different mountains, surfed different beaches, tried different jobs, moved residence frequently.

It was no different with his multiple lady friends. Nicknamed by his pals as *Flighty Felix*, he found novelty to be a powerful aphrodisiac—abhorring the mundane and the familiar.

Last Minute Fears

She decides.

Over the next hour, the consequences are considered.

She decides not.

Then, over another hour, the implications come top of mind.

Back to deciding to do it.

A "love you–love you, not" petal-pulling game.

Will she or will she not walk down the aisle today?

Landfill

Wednesday is bin day; the day a specially designed vehicle collects detritus from a week's living for its journey to the landfill site.

Sunday, a different, specially designed vehicle collects cargo for its journey. Friends and relatives watch as a life's living is lowered into the earth at another site.

Sadness[11]

The 2Cellos play the saddest of refrains, slowly, melodically drawing out my saltiest of tears.

The deep, melancholy sound of the strings produces a heart-breaking voice mirroring my own.

How can any instrument know of my pain?

The love of my life is now only a memory.

---

[11] Inspired by 2Cellos "Now We are Free"

Flowers

I'm so sorry, Sam. I was drawn in by her sparkling eyes and infectious smile.

You know that was always my weakness; the very same qualities that drew me to you all those years ago.

But I'll always love you, and I will continue to bring flowers to your gravesite.

Wash Day

The perfumed ghost on the pillows, the stained sheets, the trace of floral soap on the bath towels, the frayed emotions, the bloodshot eyes, the romantic memories, the recalled disagreements—all needing wash day; airing on the clothesline, dousing in reality: cold, wet, refreshing rain.

Now that you have left.

The Method[12]

Following "The Method," A-lister Susie prepares for her next movie. For the past month, she's been ticketing wrongfully parked cars on The Boulevard. She hooks up with Frank at Starbucks, a man who admits to adoring women in uniform.

Are they in the same movie? It's Hollywood. Frank is preparing, too.

Frugal Fran

Roasted bones always became soup with the peelings from vegetables homegrown from seed. Clothes were repaired at least once before discarding. A sweater was worn indoors rather than turning up the heat. Spending little was a wartime-learned, lifetime habit.

No one anticipated Fran's substantial estate.

---

[12] Per Wikipedia...Method Acting. The Method trains actors to use their physical, mental and emotional self in the creation of a character and stresses the way in which personal experience can fire the actors' imagination. It eschews clichés and pursues individual authenticity, and a reality deeply grounded in the given circumstances of the script.

Sirens

The small child, the sirens, the scramble for shelter, the sounds of bombs, the fear that family, friends, neighbours might not survive the night.

Many decades later, like a well-trained lab rat, he's anxious, physically shaking by the sound of sirens, even the emergency test alert on his cell phone.

Daily Routine

It was Alan's daily routine, rain or shine. Brutus took him for a brisk morning's walk while Alan dutifully followed and picked up after him.

It was not lost on Alan that this act prepared him each day for his job of dutifully caring for others at the care home.

The Front Man

On the highway, Frank always passes the car in front.

At the theatre or a lecture, he insists on sitting in the first row.

It's as though humanity must always be behind Frank, out of his purview.

Yet, while on tour, Frank plays lead guitar in front of thirty thousand.

Expenses

Stan travels for work. When in Amsterdam, he pays for sex.

Now, in Paris, he pays for lovemaking. His girlfriend joined him. He treated her to a first-class flight, the Ritz-Carlton, Dom Perignon, lobster thermidor, and a diamond.

Stan knows his future expenses for intimacy will be more like Paris.

The Waiting Room

They're all waiting

Waiting for someone
waiting for reassurance
waiting for referral
waiting for a diagnosis

Waiting to know that life
            can continue as before,
waiting for someone to say
            what they already suspect
waiting to hear
            the worst that they've imagined

For now,
        life is on hold
until told

Loyalty Programme

Simon Triliosky handed his Rewards card to the teller with a name badge, Joyce.

"Thank you, Mr. Tril…sky. May I please call you Simon?"

"Can I buy you a coffee with my rewards, Joyce?"

One hundred and fifty thousand points later, Simon was rewarded with Joyce taking his surname.

Summer Love

Lying on the warm ground, midnight skinny dippers, campers at Green Lake, have their young flesh tickled and prickled by bone-dry grass.

Peering skyward, they see satellites, planes, shooting stars, and the international space station, flashes of light moving across the sky, witnesses to summer love beneath a twinkling cosmos.

Back Then

Back then, clothes were chosen to make her look cool.

Progressively, cool migrated to sexy, then chic, and then to business-like. Her wardrobe mirrored her age and stage, but, above all, was dictated by external judgements.

At sixty, she dresses for comfort and doesn't give a toss about what others think.

Bad Day[13]

Scott was having one of his bad days.

He burnt toast. The mug held hot, dirty water–he'd not inserted a fresh coffee pod. Expletives followed to everything and anything.

Later, his mental health worker made a house call. Alexa had asked for the visit after being subjected to his abuse.

The Power of Music

Adam sits entranced, absorbed by the music, feet involuntarily tapping to its rhythm, nostrils once again smelling summer heat, hillsides of wild

---

[13] Another reference to the Amazon speaker/Alexa.

oregano, and Athena's skin. His mind's eye pictures whitewashed houses, her white diaphanous skirt, azure water, painted blue doors.

Adam's fingers tap on his phone, booking another flight.

Rebel

Brian rebelled as a teenager, as teenagers often do, but his rebellion never ended. He simply would not take instruction or advice, choosing instead to live a hermit-like, off-grid existence.

The only leader Brian tolerated was Wolf, a stray dog who adopted him, whom Brian dutifully followed on morning walks.

Role Play

We met regularly at Starbucks, our relationship developing over many coffees. On our first night together, a nude A-list actress appeared, the woman I'd come to love, no longer costumed. Her disguise was brilliant foil for relentless paparazzi and me.

When will she discover that my story is fiction, too?

Autumn

In summer warmth, love bloomed. As time passed, their affection towards each other decayed, grievances piling up like autumn maple leaves, tinged with blood and anger.

Cold, detached divorce inevitable come their third winter, as mutual frostiness resisted any melt from counselling.

Separated and bare, they each seek spring renewal.

Autumn 2

Simon, an avid inventor with a proven ability to attract angel investors, was also competitive.

He was miffed that the robot lawn mower was not his creation.

A Sunday drive through fields dotted with hay bales gave him the inspiration.

A robot to vacuum, mulch, and bag leaves.

Autumn 3

The valley floors and creeks are filled with glorious pigment: red, gold, ochre, from leaves and spent salmon; nature's last cruel painting of the season before the entire canvas is covered in winter's whiteness of frost and snow, causing all growth to slow and prepare for the green of spring.

Mrs. P.

No one–not friends nor family, the tea leaves, my horoscope, nor my palm lines have warned me to avoid the attractive, charismatic, smooth-talking you.

Now, you have me completely entranced as I follow you to your bed in Hamelin, lured by promises of bliss as Mrs. P. Piper.

Dark Shadows

Inky dark shadows fall between daylight and night– a world of fears and shapes where illicit, clandestine acts of life and death occur unseen.

It's a shadowy place where a gang member might lose his life to a rival, or a married woman might become pregnant by her lover.

Counting the Sleeps

Two more sleeps. That's all.

Eager expectations will no longer be contemplated. A voice will say, "You have arrived at your destination." Reality may or may not match what the mind has been hoping for.

When he walks off that plane, will he be everything that long-distance dating has promised?

Violet

Violet was the last of three girls. Daisy and Rosie preceded her, towering above her diminutive 5 foot 3 inches.

But Violet was not of the shrinking kind. Her parents had clearly misspelt her name.

As gang leader on the deprived estate, she became known to the police as Violent.

Release

Father's death was certainly a release, a release from his pain and the indignities that arise from infirmity.

The family assembled to hold a celebration of life.

I held my own private celebration of death and, with it, my release from the expectations and criticism that had tormented my life.

On Hold

An early morning dog walk.

Moist, easy-breathing mist. Horizon obscured by impenetrable greyness.

Beads of light reflect from each blade of grass. The finest of spray tingles the face, which, within the hour, saturates all clothing. A cock pheasant calls.

Life is unhurried, slow. Today's tasks are on hold.

Forgotten

Sounds of the oud and the ney, shimmering diaphanous skirts flowing below tummies rolling, hips swaying; the haunting call to prayer; the aromatic, spicy smell of the souk; the prickly heat of the day; gentle evening strolls; coffee as thick as river-bank mud.

Memories.

Fear of secret police momentarily forgotten.

Losing it

Brian lost his wife to cancer. Alone, bereft, liking beer and fast food, he indulged. His doctor warned of the risks, but he found no means to lose weight.

When he met a lady of interest, losing the pounds suddenly became doable.

Eejit

Amidst alcoholic blurriness, self-pitying tears, gut-wrenching discomfort, my subconscious speaks in the thick Irish brogue from the mouth of a leprechaun.

It's puzzling. I've no Irish blood.

But the self-deprecating speech of Ireland speaks to the truth and confronts me with my fallacies and shortcomings.

"Eejit."

The Lawn

Alan thought he had programmed it correctly. Perhaps an input coordinate was wrong. From upstairs, he saw splashes of yellow across an otherwise beautifully green, manicured lawn.

Rushing downstairs, he saw Rover and the robot lawn mower having a merry game of chase, neither showing regard for coordinates or daffodils.

Not Much Cop

The representatives meet annually to much fanfare—a yearly talk fest, the output of which is a creative collective of weasel words composed so they can all agree. The proverbial camel resulting from a horse designed by committee.

For small island nations, this year's COP[14] was altogether not much cop[15].

Balancing Act

It's a balancing act. Claire teeters on painful heels, holding a glass of bubbly, a small plate of nibbles, trying to look cool, not spill wine or food, measuring carefully what to say by way of meaningless small talk, wanting only to retire to the couch and snog Mr. Handsome.

---

[14] COP stands for Conference of the Parties and it often refers to the United Nations Framework Convention on Climate Change (UNFCCC) international meeting focusing on climate. COP is the main decision-making body of the UNFCCC.

[15] British, informal: not very good. She's not much cop as an actress. I'm not much cop at sports.

Diagnosis Delivered

Ill but undiagnosed, Stan lays on a hospital bed in his living room, iPad for company–music, audiobooks, video calls.

Today, two visitors stumble in with a large, unwieldy Amazon package left at his door.

They open it. OMG! It's a flatpack coffin.

Doctors have finally made their diagnosis.

DIY

Stan was a master at *do-it-yourself*.

He became a proficient cook, a mechanic, handyman, a wealthy accountant, and a bon vivant.

He lived life alone, not wanting the support of others, always wanting to do it himself.

He died alone, leaving a large legacy to a charity for single parents.

Stories

Born into a pre-determined story of deprivation, not privilege, Stan knew no silver spoons or nannies–only scraps and state benefits, with a lifetime of pre-written chapters of fights, abuse, addiction, and incarceration–intergenerational traumas on repeat.

Somehow, Stan survived, writing about its ugliness—fodder harvested for successful fictional stories.

An Old Love

I was looking to sell something online. The image popped up, reminding me of an old love. Now I cannot stop thinking about it, again and again. She's extremely pretty and a little over thirty years old but doesn't look it.

A well-designed boat; ageless to those that love them.

Patina

Everything they treasured held a patina of a former life:

She, a former sex worker.
He, once her client—twice before married.

A converted cow shed, now their home,
Filled with love,
Foster children,
Antiques and collectables
From hours spent exploring car boot sales.

Even their new jeans were stone-washed.

Migrants

Traumatised but lucky–survivors of a perilous journey from their lawless, war-ravaged homeland. Over time, language barriers fade. Their family store, open all hours, introduces ethnic foods. Success follows. Grateful, they welcome and support new arrivals.

Autumn's Traffic Lights

I'm now cautionary yellow as early autumn leaves, diminished but still holding on.

Nonchalant, carefree green days are a not-so-distant memory.

If I'm to have alarming red days, may they be palliated–I'm hoping for my decay to change yellow to brown, with a final gentle flutter to earth.

3–The Drabbles

Signs of Silliness

Stand on the Right on London's underground escalator does not mean sit on the left.

Cat's Eyes Removed on the road does not imply that felines are being blinded.

On Suspension does not mean a hanging for miscreants.

Hung Out to Dry may not be about wet laundry.

No Smoking Gun rarely involves firearms.

Open hangs on a closed door.

Watch Your Head is anatomically impossible.

Flash Fiction offers no scandalous exposure.

Moving

He was a master at harvesting nature's energy.

On the waves, he surfed beachward, in the skies, he parachuted landward.

On the ice, his land yacht slid forward or when on the sand, it rolled forward on wheels.

On the hill, he snowboarded downward.

When an illness confined him to a wheelchair, he moved his fingers, writing fast-moving thrillers or moved the joystick, terrorising staff at the rehabilitation centre with the wheelchair's speed.

Knock on the Door

There was a time when a whole family would share a single bathroom. In so doing, each household member appreciated they had an impact on others. A knock on the door made clear that other humans had needs.

Today, first world inhabitants live without the need to share, in homes that do not force them to accommodate others.

Is it any wonder that civilised dialogue and mutual respect are on the wane?

Big Hitter

Heads are turned by a red, low-cut, sultry, slit dress, exposing leg and ample cleavage. Her eyes and smile reel them in.

It's a company year-end drinks party, a bull ring with only one celeb, the conspicuous centrepiece of a matador huddle.

Despite this year's lowest pay grade, tonight, she's declared she's a big hitter. Workmates politely sip their wine, jealously speculating as to who she will go home with at the party's end.

Now is Not the Time

At high school: "Susie! Now is not the time to daydream."

After school: "Now is not the time, sweetheart. Can't you see Mummy is busy making supper?"

On the weekend: "Now is not the time, sweetheart. Daddy wants to watch the game."

One evening: Susie slips away to see a boy who has the time.

At the clinic: "Now is not the time for pills. You are already ten weeks along."

Skipping Stones

It is a warm, windless summer evening, high tide—water's surface waveless, calm, reflective. Sounding a gentle wish-wash at the shoreline. John is at the water's edge picking up skipping stones.

For his first throw, he says, "This is for you, Mum." The stone skips five times.

"This is for you sweetheart." His wife. Stone skips four times.

"This is for you, Dad." Skips twice.

"This is for you, Mellissa." His first love. Skips seven times.

For his final stone, he says, "And, this one is for me." Skips once.

John wondered if he'd discovered a new tool for measuring love.

First Massage

His visual world is through a porthole—a small circle of floor and portions of feet shooed in red canvas, a view made smaller when she applies pressure to his shoulders.

Constrained, feeling, thinking–no one has explored his nakedness like this before, not even energetic lovers.

While the masseuse kneads body parts, he's trying to resist fantasizing about the red-shoed woman, becoming anxious about the stirrings in his groin.

"Please roll over."

Cemetery

I thought our torrid, extra-marital affair was long buried.

Two decades ago, I'd ritually placed our secret letters beneath a rose bush at the bottom of the garden, a rose with petals as cherry red as her lipstick and thorns as sharp as her wit.

But with the internet, nothing is interred.

I got a phone call, the voice sounding strangely familiar.

She claims I'm her biological father and wants my DNA to prove it.

Moving On

She shuffled through the security protocol, stooped, burdened with something weighty. A shoulder bag, a carry-on suitcase, and her dignity were all the possessions that she carried as she boarded.

The business class seat offered spacious luxury, champagne on tap, an attentive stewardess, and time to reflect.

The journey was now feeling less of an adventure, more like a rash decision. A new job, new country, new relationships.

What could go wrong?

Her Thighs

The pianist was playing easy-listening jazz on the grand piano. The soft, leather hotel lounge seat was as low as the whiskey now in Adam's glass. The server noticed that he might need a refill.

At eye level, her thighs approached, just barely concealed by a black form-fitting skirt.

From that moment, Adam knew he would be prepared to give up everything in order to be in their company forever.

The Corset[16]

I felt the tension as the lady's maid pulled and tugged my laces. It was an onerous task, squeezing, lifting, and holding her ladyship's very fulsome form before her other colourful garments were placed atop.

My role in this charade was to provide a voyeur's peak at a well-presented bosom–an essential pretense to attract a suitor of sufficient means to keep her ladyship in the manner to which she had become accustomed.

Such a presentation, together with a handheld, ornate eye mask, was designed to invoke mystery and intrigue at the ball and help secure her ladyship's desired future.

Headwinds

It's a safe choice. Headwinds do not penetrate this deep into the protected bay. The anchor is set. It holds firm when tested against the pull imposed by the motor.

Calm descends. Time and physical movement are unhurried. Survival, physical exertion against the blustery squalls become a memory.

---

[16] Shannon at Author's Only Collective suggested telling a story from a unique viewpoint like an inanimate object. This was my response.

It's a time to breathe, reflect, feed the hunger, sleep.

Tomorrow, rested, nourished, ready for a repeat, he and his craft will again do battle.

Memories

It's early autumn. The mid-morning sun streaks through the oaks, leaves partially dressed for fall, some green but many golden yellow, burnt orange, bright red. As the gentle breeze moves them, the sunlight flutters on its path through the blinds onto the closed eyes of the resting figure on the couch.

Behind those closed eyes, fluttering light gives sparkle to the azure, blue water. A woman is running barefoot on the sand to greet him.

"Here's your tea, Grandpa."

He opens his eyes, reaches for his tea, and wonders if she, like her Grandma, will run to her soul mate.

Earring Stud

It had been an evening of choreographed anticipation before her final denouement at D's place. "Meet me for dinner after work at Le Clarence," he said.

Dinner was a slow, no expense spared, multi-course seduction. Slightly tipsy, she followed him to his flat afterwards as if he were the Pied Piper.

Their coupling, eager, sweaty and satisfying, made all the more so because of the elaborate build-up that he had orchestrated.

Now home, Colette had time for a quick shower and a change of clothes before she headed to the Metro. It was then she realised that she had lost an earring stud.

At lunch that day, D called. "My wife wants to know where the gold stud came from, Colette. I'm now off to have my left ear pierced."

Risk and Reward

Tom did not want to live alone. He struggled with social anxiety, especially when it came to women.

He was uncomfortable sitting in bars, hoping to randomly meet someone. Swiping right seemed too risky.

He noticed people walking their dogs seemed to have an affinity for each other. But he did not want to include a dog in his life.

Then he realised that people who smoked tended to huddle just outside of their office buildings on their smoke break.

Tom took up smoking. The risk of early death by lung cancer seemed a reasonable pay-off to avoid loneliness, which also shortens life.[17]

Bedtime Conversations

In the dark wee hours, Brian spoke to someone unseen in a language like the African Khoisan—comprising clicks and grunts. From time to time, he clearly disagreed, and a horse-like whinny could be heard in response.

As time passed, Brian's conversations became more insistent. In his final days, he seemed increasingly desperate, disagreeing more frequently, his tone defiant, until on one fateful night, Brian lost all the arguments and forever fell silent.

---

[17] In 2019, Scientific American reported: 'Loneliness has been estimated to shorten a person's life by 15 years, equivalent in impact to being obese or smoking 15 cigarettes per day.' (https://blogs.scientificamerican.com/observations/loneliness-is-harmful-to-our-nations-health/)

Time's Up

Sam's life was an untimely affair.

Born two months early, Sam thereafter lived life by the mantra–*Just in Time*,–meaning he was habitually late when handing in assignments, for appointments, social events, and work.

When rushed to compensate for his tardiness, he spilt coffee going into meetings and received speeding tickets on the way to appointments.

Sam struggled with timely decision-making, including marriage. When married, he regretted that he was too old to become a father.

His long-suffering wife endured until, for only the second time, Sam was incredibly early.

At fifty-seven, he died from a fatal heart attack.

Choice[18]

For much of the world's population, the true miracle of modern life is neither AI nor technological innovation; it is individual choice.

For many, it is no longer a crime to ignore parents, the Church, inherited authority, presumptive gender

---

[18] Written in the light of the many news stories of illegals crossing the English Channel.

designations, or class-defined mores. But in the face of choice, individual decisions can be both very daunting and risky.

Sometimes, decisions can result in drowning in the Channel en route to an imagined better life.

Downsizing

Diane's new residence is going to be only half as big.

Widowed, she must choose what to take and what not. She considers each item, thinking not of its commercial value but of its associated memory–a vase from Greece where she had a short summer romance, a pocket watch passed down from her doting father, a pressed flower from her wedding bouquet, a night table made by her late husband.

How can she decide which memory she must now leave behind? New owners will only see the object's utility, not the hidden, embedded significance.

Is it downsizing or curated amnesia?

Noises

Almost asleep. Eyes closed. Auditory senses extra alert.

The only noise is from a fridge and a gently whirling ceiling fan. But somehow, Alan's quite sure the sounds are voices. He strains to hear what is being said.

"Oh dear, oh dear, oh dear," says the fan.

"Phooone, phooone, phooone," says the fridge.

He gets up to find a text message.

Alan's aged mother, on the other side of the country, has passed.

Best Laid Plans

Brian purposely chose a snowy winter's day, but the weather had degraded into a total whiteout. Although road, field and sky were indistinguishable, he drove on. The car slid into a ditch, and now Brian needed a tow truck.

So much for fresh snow covering his tracks. He needed to move the stuck vehicle before the cops tagged or attempted to retrieve it.

Brian had not yet disposed of the body.

Prescription

Susie was seeing Roxanne, her alternative therapist. She'd been seeing her on and off for a couple of years. Ever since her partner John left some three months ago, Susie felt listless, anxious, sleep-deprived, and depressed. Roxanne listened to her story and wrote her a prescription:

- *Buy or use a Magic Wand daily before sleep, or*
- *Hire Colin (404-676-3000) for protein injection—or both.*
- *Make a follow-up appointment with me in a couple of months.*

Dead End

I retreat to a room without light, sliding the meagre bolt I installed yesterday. On the bed, sweat and tears slip along my bruised skin, silently entering wounds like salty water torture.

Will my husband recover? If he does, I fear my life will end violently.

If he does not, then this self-imposed incarceration will be replaced by another the authorities impose.

First a Kiss

Suzzi painted cityscapes in bright colours: architectural statements, yellow cabs, umbrellas, neon signs.

Then, a frequent visitor said, "These paintings are not life. They show bright, shiny things. Where is the feeling?"

Suzzi, realising his truth, went to kiss him. "Be warned," he cautioned. "Love and new life first begin with a kiss."

Thereafter, her brush strokes recorded what she felt.

Nine months later, she was entirely consumed with a new life.

The Importance of Hair

Dan still remembers when the first signs of dark body hair were celebrated amongst his teenage peer group as an indication of their emerging maleness and virility, an important rite of passage.

Now, years later, Dan uses razors and depilatory creams to remove any signs of Neanderthal hirsuteness and keeps a distinctive bald head like that of Yul Brynner.

As a porn star, hair is unnecessary as evidence of his masculinity.

Holes

At the veteran's care home, Stan sat every day, staring out the window. His gnarly hands rested on his substantial middle, and although big, they could not hide the holes in his favourite sweater.

Holes from the past, holes from cigarette ash, holes that reminded him of holes in the fuselage, holes that killed his comrades.

Stan had trouble living with survivor's guilt all these years, vividly remembering each of his crew mates lost on that night mission.

But he knew it was not long now before he, too, would be lowered into a dirt hole to meet his mates, through disease and advanced age rather than by enemy bullets.

Pockets

As a very small boy, objects in Granddad's pockets were a wonder.

There was always his red pocketknife and a white handkerchief, plus other treasures he'd picked up: a hand-forged nail, a rusty screw, perhaps an old penny or a tactile stone.

He delighted in producing the items and telling his young grandson some fictitious story based on the object.

When Granddad died, the boy would keep his grandfather's red knife in his pocket.

In Hot Water

She'd become increasingly suspicious. His frequent use of the gym seemed odd; she cancelled their membership last week.

"Hello, Honey. I'm home. I've had a workout at the gym. I'm just going to take a shower."

She'd unplugged the on-demand hot water heater before he got home.

"What the …! Honey, I'm not getting any hot water."

"There's going to be a lot more things you won't be getting from now on."

A Night with the Boys

3:42 AM. Steve is tossing. Turning. Trying to escape his own body. His stomach was vocal about its discomfort. Painful, furry teeth sit uneasily within a mouth of sandpaper. The sinus beneath one eye is pressing uncomfortably on his cheekbone. Was it the curry or the copious jugs of local brew? Thankfully, he stayed over in a motel.

When is the café open?

He needs strong coffee. And a full English breakfast.

First Impression

I'd seen the face before. I was sure I'd left-swiped back then, but this time something piqued my interest. Swipe right.

At a local café, while seated at the table, I see determination, confidence, striding towards me, as if approaching an important job interview.

Thirty minutes later, relaxed, smiling, sipping their flat white, I saw beyond their visage and confirmed I'd been wrong the first time. This encounter appears to hold much promise.

Synchronicity

Susan's newest home appliance purchase promises novelty, utility and a one-year warranty. Thirteen months later, the device fails to work. Its repair proves not cost-effective, so Susan discards it and replaces it with a newer model.

Full of hope, their union was formalized. No warranty other than publicly expressed vows and a pre-nuptial. Thirteen years later, novelty over, the partnership fails.

Relationship counselling proves ineffective, and Susan is replaced by a new, younger model.

One Letter

Twenty-six letters declaring expressions of love; declaring expressions of interest.

Twenty-six letters that advise rejection; that advise acceptance.

Twenty-six letters that record *not guilty*; that record incarceration.
Twenty-six letters of written journalistic news; of written response to the editor.

Twenty-six letters that document one's wishes; that document death.

Twenty-six letters to write one's thoughts; to write a decision.

Twenty-six letters to write one letter—then post it.

Today, online. Yesterday, in the postbox.

The Passing of Time

Earth's rotation on its axis, or its orbit around the sun, has nothing to do with it.

Driving to the vacation cabin, the journey feels endlessly long. Driving home seems to take no time at all.

It's the anticipation of the destination that alters our perception of time. The child's *Are we there yet?* says it all.

Ageing, too, is an unwelcome destination, leaving us with memories that feel like yesterday.

Code Flags

A street of terraced, Victorian houses; homes and gardens attached cheek by jowl to each other, just as the lives of its residents inevitably become intertwined over time.

At ground level, high fences and walls provide privacy between gardens.

From first-floor windows everything is visible, including the ubiquitous backyard washing lines.

Mrs. Jones and Mr. Simmons exploited this as a means of communication–when Mrs. Jones hung out white coloured washing, with a single pair of bright red underwear, it was as an all-clear signal–Mr. Jones was absent. When more colourful garments were drying, it meant caution–stay away.

Intergenerational Trauma

As time passes, my reflection has become less and less tolerable.
It is complicated.

I hate the memories triggered by the reflection. And the more I see, the more I dislike myself, as I do my father.

One day recently, in a fit of rage, I removed all the household mirrors and smashed them to pieces. It was a cathartic outburst. I no longer see my deceased father.

I'm growing a beard. Will this be enough to differentiate me from my father? At least I won't see him when I shave.

I wonder if my son will feel the same.

Welcome

Rodger had miraculously survived the night—or was it two or three? He had no way of knowing. His last recall was the blinding headlights and the screech of tires.

Where was he?

By virtue of a slit in the wrappings around his head, he could just see glimpses of a figure. *Was it a nurse? Or was it an angel? Or the devil?*

There was something odd about the figure's ears. *Was that a stethoscope—or horns?*

And what was the figure holding? *Was it a torture prong—or a temperature probe?*

"Good morning, Mr. Johns. Welcome to Saint Inns."

Wet Dreams

Through the pre-dawn greyness, the sun had yet to bring forth daylight while birds chirped to warn away competitors, to woo mates, and perhaps to pass along the gossip of the day or simply to tell their avian tales.

The bird's noisy chatter was Bob's alarm clock. His foggy mind slowly awakened, clinging to remnants of his dream–a vivid, arousing fantasy of the past, of defiant and submissive ladies and daring, handsome rakes.

As reality emerged, he looked down and felt a warm flush of embarrassment.

He hoped the washing machine would erase both the evidence and his self-consciousness.

4–The Poems

Hat

If I grew my hair long
ponytail tied
or in one lobe
put an earring inside

If I chose
grubby clothes
or wore flip-flops
for my toes

If I learned a few chords
plucking on some string
or fingered a keyboard
while trying to sing

If I did all these things
or tried even three
Would I be more creative
Or would you disagree

If I donned a fedora
or puffed on a joint
Would it improve my meter
Or would my rhymes still disappoint.

River

Oh, to be like a river
to have the river's emotions
clear and cool
determined and reflective

Babbling musically
shimmering, glistening
in its happiness
but always moving incessantly
against all obstructions
towards its objective

Other times
becoming a pool
of reflective, deep calm
silent and thoughtful
despite surely knowing
of a riffle or two
around the bend

Oh, to be so contained.

Love's Name

I like it so very much
that you know my name
not just the name
the world calls me
or the one my mother used
when I transgressed
but a name that is in a language
from no known place
yet is in every place that we inhabit
the name that sums up
who I am in this world
the name that only you and I speak
the name that only
intimacy can give
that says so much about
our journey, our joy, our pain
and pervades my entire being.

Did You

Did you sleep alone last night
Was your bed warmed by another
Were you kept awake by thoughts of me
Or did you take a lover

Did he love you well enough
Did you think of me in slumber
Will you join with him again
Now he's figured out your number

I slept alone myself last night
And jealous if you shared your bed
I'm crazy to have gone away
And want to be with you instead

The sheets are cold with aching soul
At morning's rise, the lonely bed
With no skin to reach or heat to feel
Past nights reside inside my head

Did you sleep alone last night
Was your bed warmed by another
Were you kept awake by thoughts of me
Or did you take a lover.

Coal Black

In the coal black
silence

a maudlin echo
a cello sounding
heartfelt grief

an unrealised life
trickles down
onto a damp pillow

then dawn chirps
out the silence

we simply
carry on.

Tethered towards Extinction

We live
this life
leashed like an IV drip
to the nearest power outlet
lest our screens blacken to low battery

Phone plugged into the grid
we, too, become recharged

In touch
befriended but
without hands
without nuance
eyes downcast to the screen
unaware of welcoming strangers
walking past

Australopithecus tended their fires
to tell stories, to survive
we tend our Facebook, TikTok

One provides warmth
the other cerebral solace

One fosters connection, procreation

The other political polarization
division, untruths
low fecundity

Do we become
thus, a species
critically endangered?

Time Traveler

We're time travelers
at any given moment
we're perhaps 10 or 30 years younger
remembering so vividly
how it was
then finding out that frighteningly
we're inhabiting older bones

How did that happen?

Steed

Long ago, he sat astride his steed

a shiny, black, hot-blooded, Arabian

Later, his charger became an equine-badged
red, rag-top, chick magnet
302 cubic inches of pulsating testosterone

Now, his grey ponytail is the only mane
recalling past hippie days
and some semblance of retained virility

In life's final insult to his masculinity
he rides a puny, three-wheeled scooter.

Knight

Along the banks
between reeds and trees
and in the pools of the river
he keeps peering
hoping to see
a lost saviour of maidens
cloaked in glimmering steel
a knight, brightly adorned
with colourful symbols
of past victories

Sadly
the water
returns only rippled
wrinkled images
of a tired and weary warrior
minus his armour and scabbard
sporting a cane for a sword
and the latest badge of age
an electronic accelerometer
lest he should stumble and fall.

Shadows

In silver moonlight
black silhouetted headstones
eclipse their buried mounds
shadowed trees lie prone
on the path I walk

My body, a charcoal shape
projected towards the darkness
precedes me
leaving in my wake
the brightness
of my existence
forever dimmed...

Worry

It's become a time of worry

maybe it's my bad breath
or the loss of some function or other
a capacity no longer usable
without a consequence

Is that irritation
a sign of something sinister?
is the food eaten a cause of some malady
or just extra weight?

And those friends of mine
peers, all of them
news of them might imply
the coming news of me

Then there's the wider issue
of falsehoods
spouted from the mouths
or in the tweets of those voted in
was history so full of lies?
or do we just now
hear of it incessantly

And, of course, there's always
the bloody weather to fret about
it's surely now more extreme
than living memory recalls

(but in this case, scientists give credence
for worry)

Being older
there's so much time available to worry
time to reflect
on how it is now
versus how it was then

Chronologically, the body is older
but perhaps the brain is not wiser
beneath hair loss
with never-before-acknowledged organs
To be concerned about acting strange

So many causes for worry
how long is there left to do this or that
how long to love
worry is everywhere

And in due course
it will become too late for worries
except for one
and then I'll be done.

Night Silence

A pillowed ear hears
wump, wump, wump
sixty-five beats per minute

a cold ear hears
the low hum, hum
of furnace, fan or fridge

Brain
ignore both ears

But no amount of concentration
can dispel the unwanted intrusion

Sleep
so damned elusive
now the worries start

Did I lock the front door?
The car?

Damn!! the bladder calls

Is there no end
to this stupidity?

Relent

Get up
make coffee,
write poetry.

Our Past Lives

Shut tight eyelids
clouds of pale yellow and white
degrading to pinprick stars
residual activity
within the retina
not exactly a roar
of the Metro lion
but an intro nonetheless
before the movie begins
before images of you appear
selected retakes
of our lives
screened
as sleep awaits.

Pseudo-Science

Of course, the wretchedness is real
like some malady from mosquitoes
or viruses too small to see
or environmental poisons drifting on air
or ingested off surfaces of tasty morsels
but to ascribe the protagonist to wheat belly
or to some nefarious allergy
may simply be a means to invoke a placebo effect
in the face of non-existent science
but if it works, if discomfiture is less
what is there to disagree?

Tired

Long, long ago
a boy so tired
tired of trying to be a man

What maketh man?
strong, serious?

Now a man
or just an old boy?

Tired of holding
the boy at bay

the boy who
wants to play
fragile, frivolous.

Perhaps

Perhaps
I shouldn't have been born at all

A mere accident of birth
outcome of one too many therapeutic
couplings
solace
following horrors of war

Ultimately, I joined a demographic
destined to be a newly named herd

Consummate consumers
wanton waste producers

Followers of Chicagoan
trickle-down economics
free markets
free enterprise

Peace and free love

Creators of satellites
social media
container shipping

GMO, GPS
MRI, Apollo eleven
iPhones and the pill

Plus, way too much CO_2

Destroyers
Of the Berlin wall
polio, smallpox
coral reefs
climate, habitat

And much, much more

We're now blamed
for practically everything
that is most often
simply a tragedy
of the commons

Good for one
bad for everyone

A tragedy of progress
self-preservation, self-fulfillment
indulgence, ignorance
with co-lateral damage
economic inequality and
other unimagined externalities

Perhaps war or pestilence
with death on a massive scale
will force our attention
away from post-truth

gross nostalgia and
the loss of all faith in reason

For those who survive
social science and
behavioural psychologists
will be sorely needed
to re-direct populism

And our animal herd instincts

Meanwhile
we can but pray that
science nerds
will solve
the seemingly unsolvable

And that politicians will listen
will comply
and apply

For our
demographic herd
dementia, MAID[19], oblivion
will arrive soon enough

Now seen as pariahs
our legacy will not be
so easily undone

Indeed
I should not have been born at all.

---

[19] MAID = Medical Assistance in Dying.

There

When uncle touched me *there*.

When nobody listened
When nobody believed
When nobody acted

When trust was but spume
   ripped from the waves in a ferocious gale
When calmer seas never return
When confidence drowns

When I'm forever disbelieved
When all men appear to leer
   presumed guilty by virtue of gender

My life diminishes, no longer thrives

Until someone listens
Until the judiciary believes
Until the courts act.

Oh! Canada

A time to sit by a fire
a time to reflect
read a good book
sip hot chocolate or eggnog
make stews and soups
cuddle the dog, your loved one
appreciate the sun when it shines
breathe easily the cooler air
make snow angels, snowmen
think about spring, summer
as you put on snow tyres
think of warm sun and sand
as you don scarf and gloves
but mostly think
this is Canada
land of winter joy.

Publishing History

Vines Leaves Press.com (50 Give or Take)

Lemons *Raise Up*
Mirror be Damned *The Lawn*
The Power of Music *Release*
Finer Grind *On Hold*

Paragraph Planet

First Impressions *Two Days*
First Massage *The Passing of Time*
Moving *Balancing Act*
Now Is not The Time *Big Hitter*
Synchronicity *Moving*
Cemetery *Pockets*

Fiftywordstories.com

Landfill

101Words.org

Time's Up *Skipping Stones*

365tomorrows.com

Lost

Roi Faineant Press

Book Box   *Mrs. P.*

Suddenly, and Without Warning

Until the Next Time

The Rye Whiskey Review

Until the Next Time

About the Author

Before qualifying to be an engineer, there were hints of my interest in creative writing—a poem here, a short creative piece there, usually written to meet some course requirement.

For the following thirty-six years, my working life required me to write proposals seeking higher-level, technical and financial approval. Those documents were always structured in a consistent format to suit corporate processes. Along with the proposals were detailed, line by line, instructions for the execution of what was proposed. Occasionally, there was a need to write longer reports outlining the analysis and the technical and financial rationale for a particular course of action: so-called *Technical Writing*.

Once retired, and in stark contrast to my working life, I sought out creative art forms, pottery, sculpture and free verse poetry. I found the freedom to write without strict rules compelling.

In 2022, I discovered Flash Fiction. Specifically, the genre of very short stories –

micro-fiction–written to an exact limit of, for example, 50 or 101 words. I became attracted to the genre. It was (is) fun to write a very short story and then move on to write another one.

This book reflects my writing passion. Within these pages are predominantly adult-themed short stories. Some stories qualify as *Dribble* (50 words), *Drabble* (100 words) and *Flash* (up to 500 or more words).

Compared to my first book, I've included rather more footnotes this time by way of explaining the stories.

The stories reflect my wry observations, sense of humour, and curiosity about the world around me.

It is an evocative, playful compendium of stories and poetry that speaks to the nature of our lives, its highs and lows, our pain and joy, our fantasies, life's quirks and realities and even a bit of life's silliness.

Printed in Great Britain
by Amazon